In Wildness Is The Preservation Of The World

Henry David Thoreau

ACKNOWLEDGEMENTS

I want to thank my daughters Becca and Jessie, the two eternal lights in my life; my wonderful family; the late Barbara Clarke, co-founder of DreamCatcher Wild Horse and Burro Sanctuary; Mara Eriel for her extraordinary help getting this book in published form and to the wild horses who continue to inspire me.

INTRODUCTION

I am an American mustang. My life began twenty years ago in the high desert…….

MY FIRST YEAR

The dun colored mare emerged from a grove of junipers. She moved cautiously, sniffing the air, eyes searching for possible danger. When all seemed safe, she nickered towards the opening in the trees. The new foal, black with a small white mark on his face, slowly moved out through the opening and trotted over to his mother. The small band of horses welcomed their newest member. Together they moved to the watering hole. Illuminated by a rising moon, the stallion watched as the band drank until it was time to move on into the darkening night. A night filled with falling stars which startled the new foal. He stopped and stomped his small hoof. His mother nickered softly to reassure him. As they moved off, the only sound that could be heard were their hooves travelling over the rough ground. The foal's first night. The peace of this first day would only last a short time, but would remain a powerful memory.

TWO YEARS LATER

Through the cloud of dust, a band of wild horses could be seen. Circling above them, a helicopter continued to push the horses forward. The sound of fear could be heard over the monster hovering overhead. They continued to run even though exhaustion was overtaking the old and the very young.   Many stumbled but the machine continued to push them forward. Ahead of them a horse could be seen approaching the band. The wild ones ran toward him not knowing he was a Judas horse. He was there to lead them to their fate. Ahead was a long chute, but before they realized there was no way out they were forced into a small holding pen. Chaos caused the horses to run into the fences trying to find a way out. One did, a young black stallion with a small white mark on his face had escaped. He had broken away from the group and disappeared into the nearby hills. It took the government employees some time before they realized the stallion had escaped. There would be another opportunity and the helicopter had already left to round up more horses.

On a ridge behind an outcropping, the young stallion watched his family trapped in the corral. He nickered softly. He waited there until his family was loaded onto the trucks. They spoke to him as they moved away. For the first time, he was alone. This young mustang would learn to adapt to the high desert environment. It would serve him well in the years to come.

TEN YEARS LATER

The black mustang, with the now famous white mark on his face, was now a mature stallion with a band of his own. His once black coat showed the scars he had earned keeping his band together. He was once again being forced to run along the desert floor chased by that now familiar helicopter. He was running behind the group trying to figure a way out for them, but it was too late. The chute was visible along with the trap that would take them away from their freedom. He knew what he had to do. Once inside the corral, he kept going toward the far end to make his escape. Those working shouted in amazement. The employee, who worked as an independent contractor, voiced his amazement. "Whew, did you see that?" The second employee standing nearby seconded that statement.

"That's not something you see every day in this job. He's going to be tough to catch. He scratched his head thinking out loud. "Sure looks like that horse that got away a few years back. Just a lot bigger!"

They finished loading up the frightened horses and dismantled the chute and corral.

"Well, maybe next time." The employee said with displeasure. "Maybe next time."

The lone stallion had now lost two families. This time he didn't look back but wandered the high desert searching for any wild ones who might still be out there.

Over the years, the removal of the wild horses occurred once every few years, but now the pace of the captures had quickened. Constant pressure from special interests together with local, state and government agencies were determined to see every last one removed.

PRESENT DAY

When the last light had left the sky, the stallion approached the corrals at the government holding facility. His years of escaping his captors had taught him well. He could hear the whinnying of the captive horses. Suddenly, he kicked at the fence until it gave way allowing the horses to push through the opening. The sound of their hooves could be heard in the darkness. After they had been freed, the stallion followed. He stopped at the top of the hill overlooking the facility, threw is head, looked back and vanished into the night.

The following morning, two government employees approached the holding corral. Both stopped when they saw the empty corral and the damaged fence.

One of the employees asked the other, "How the heck do you think this happened?" The other employee had removed his hat and threw it on the ground. He kicked the ground and started shouting and waving his arms. He continued to kick the ground out of frustration.

At the local diner, Samuel, an elderly Native American and well known resident of this high desert community, nodded to Gus, the owner, and took a seat. The diner was a welcome sight to the few residents who lived in the area. All the news started and ended at the diner. Gus, who had been talking to a small group of friends in another booth approached Samuel.

"Did you hear about all the horses that broke out of the holding corral down the road?"

Laughing, "Must have been a beautiful sight. One guess as to how it happened?"

A smiling Gus, "News like that gets around here pretty quick. Are you suggesting that old mustang had something to do with it?"

"Yes, I am." Samuel responded. "But he's bought himself a whole lotta trouble now. The government wants all those wild ones gone for good and they won't quit till they get them."

Thoughtfully, Gus said, "Now that would be a shame. I've only seen him a few times in the last few years, but I like knowing he's out there. This place wouldn't be the same without the wild horses."

Through the window of the diner Gus and Samuel are engaged in conversation. Outside, Gus's dog, Bella and several other dogs played in the parking lot. This scene had played out many times over the years, but something was different this time. Gus and Sam were unaware how their lives would be changed by this one horse.

A few days later the stallion watched behind a distant tree as the escaped horses were loaded onto the transport. The horses stomped and whinnied as the truck pulled away. Their short- lived freedom gone once more. But once more the stallion had escaped their grasp. The government employees who helped capture the horses discussed the stallion.

"He won't be turning them loose again. He's not in this group but we'll find him. Send the copter out later to find him."

"I don't know. He's probably long

gone by now." He looked up toward the nearby hills, "I'm through chasing him. This time we're going to get him. I don't care how long it takes.

"Don't be so sure. He's been hiding out in these mountains a long time. He's a legend in these parts." They spoke as both of them looked up into the hills. The stallion moved away from the scene below. He found a safe place behind an outcropping and watched the truck as it grew smaller in the distance. He heard a final whinny. As he moved away from the capture site, he stopped and looked back one last time.

2

The truck carrying the horses pulled up to the pumps outside Gus's diner. He approached the driver who rolled down his window. "Could you fill it up?" Gus responded while he gave the truck the once over, "Sure." After he placed the nozzle into the gas tank, Gus wandered over towards the back of the truck. He ran his hand along the side of the truck while he whispered inaudibly. He stopped suddenly. A horse inside the trailer made eye contact with him. Under normal conditions he wouldn't have been startled but this encounter was different. It was as if time had stopped. Gus didn't know it yet but it was a life changing moment. He had no idea how long he'd been standing there until he heard the driver's voice.

"Cleaning out this area. Got everything but an older stallion, but we'll be back later. Hey, how much do I owe you?"

Gus, "That will be fifty bucks. Care to make a wager you don't catch him?"

 The driver handed Gus the money and proceeded to start up the truck. He leaned out his window and with a grin said, "From what I heard, I might lose that bet. Thanks again."

Gus watched the truck pull away, and continued to watch until the truck disappeared down the road. He reached down to rest his hand on Bella's head and raised his eyes toward the nearby mountains.

"So, they left you behind."

He stood for a long time with Bella at his side looking off into the distance while the sun set over the horizon. At the same time the lone stallion whinnied one last time before he disappeared into the night. Only his hoof beats could be heard on the hard ground. Gus and Bella went back into the diner. No one there but the two of them. He reached down to pat her head and said, "What do you say we go out and look for some fossils tomorrow. Maybe we'll run into that horse. Like to see how he's doing out there." Bella barked in agreement. Gus turned off the lights as he and Bella headed into the back of the diner. A routine they had repeated many times. Gus had lived alone at the diner for many years. He had thought about leaving a few times, but the high desert community which numbered less than one hundred had become his family. He had never married. He had accepted the life he had chosen without regret.

3

The following morning Gus opened the diner to his friends who came by every day for breakfast. They took their usual seat and exchanged greetings. Their conversation was interrupted by a woman none of them had seen before. She was an older woman dressed for the outdoors. She carried a large well-worn canvas bag over her shoulder. She picked up the snow globe which contained a horse mounted on a rock that was sitting by the register. Gus had wandered over. "Pretty isn't it?" He watched as she shook the globe.

"It's lovely." She handed the globe back to him.

"Now, what can I get you?"

Rose introduced herself and placed her order, "I'd like to fill up this thermos and get a couple bottles of water since I'll be out all day."

Gus perked up, "Sure. First time up here? This diner is the only place within 50 miles so you might want to get some sandwiches to go with that coffee."

Rose smiled, "Thank you that sounds great. Yes, it is my first time visiting this area. Any ideas where I might find some fossils?"

"I sure do. I'm an amateur rock hunter myself." He scratched his head. "I've got a map here somewhere. By the way, my name is Gus. I'm the owner of this place." Gus pulled out a map from under the counter. He continued to have a conversation with Rose, and didn't notice two of his friends watching them with interest. Daniel, one of Gus's oldest friends, nudged the other one and both laughed. Meanwhile, Gus continued his conversation. "Just follow this route along the base of the mountain. You'll find some, just need patience. Not many folks know about this spot."

Rose responded, "Well, time is all

I've got now since I retired. Thank you again for the information." Rose picked up the snow globe. "Any chance of seeing a few of these?"

Gus, "There aren't many left, but I do know at least one old stallion is still out there. Sure would like to see him one more time before they catch him."

"Why do they want to catch him?"

"I think a handful of folks have other plans for this part of the country." Gus responded. "Shame though. Now why don't you have yourself a seat while I get your order."

Gus went into the kitchen to prepare her sandwiches. He found himself humming but didn't know why.

Rose took a seat at the counter and took out her journal. When Gus returned with her thermos and sandwiches, she handed him her money. "Thank you for your help. Really appreciate your suggestions." Rose left the diner and got into her truck. Gus, along with his friends, watched as she drove away. Gus noticed his friend, Daniel, smiling at him.

"What's got you smiling?" Gus asked.

Daniel responded with a wink, "Haven't seen you that talkative in quite some time."

Gus, avoiding his remark, "Might get an afternoon thunderstorm. Should have warned her about that."

Daniel, with a big grin, "Gee, maybe you should go out there later and check on her."

Gus had lived a quiet life in this high desert community. He wasn't sure why he was so interested in this stranger for many had passed through before. The last couple of days had proved unsettling for Gus. His normal routine had been disrupted by that horse in the trailer and now this woman who had appeared this morning. He was puzzled and when his friends had left, he sat by the window for quite some time until he heard Bella barking. He shook his head to clear his thoughts, "Ok girl I'm coming "

4

The stallion had been at the watering hole for a short time. It was surrounded by large junipers, but he still had to be careful. In the reflection of the water, he was suddenly startled by the image of a woman standing on top of an overhang above the pool. He immediately moved away from the water and into the grove of junipers. Rose had seen the stallion before it had moved out of view. Speaking to herself, "I wonder if that is the horse Gus was talking about" No sooner had the words left her mouth the stallion had disappeared. It was as if he had vanished into thin air. The wind had picked up a bit and a dust cloud had formed in the distance. Rose was mesmerized by the sights and sounds, even the air had changed. Now the dust cloud had changed shape. She wasn't sure she could trust her eyes. The cloud had become an image of a small herd of horses. To Rose, they looked like ghosts. By now her breathing had quickened. But, as quickly as the image had appeared, it was gone and so was the stallion. Rose asked herself, "What did I just see?" After a few minutes, she gathered up her things and descended down toward the watering hole where she had seen the horse. She approached with caution. Nothing was disturbed except for a few hoof prints. She followed them until they disappeared on the rocky surface. Rose then walked toward the area where the image of the ghost horses had appeared. There were no tracks. Rose once again spoke to herself, "Where could they have gone? Not a good sign, old girl. You're talking to yourself and seeing things that aren't there." She sat down on a nearby rock and took out her journal and began writing furiously. She didn't notice the ominous clouds forming in the distance.

The storm brewing outside Gus's diner caught his attention. He looked down at his watch and then spoke to Bella, who was sitting by the door. "You're thinking what I'm thinking? Yeah, let's go check on her." Bella barked and pushed the door open.

Gus hung a closed sign in the window, locked the door and the two of them headed for his pickup. He held the door open and Bella jumped in. The two of them drove off into the darkening sky. Gus parked the truck in one of the spots he had suggested to Rose. He moved through the scrub until he came upon the ledge Rose had previously occupied. It was then he spotted her truck. He was unaware that he was being observed by the stallion. This wise older mustang had learned to protect himself over the years. He stood so still only his breathing could be heard but his eyes were riveted on Gus who had just climbed back into his truck. Gus made his way over to Rose's truck and he and Bella got out. He realized she didn't hear him, but she turned around when she heard Bella barking.

Gus, "Everything okay? We were getting a little worried when we saw the storm headed this way. They can come up real fast out here."

Rose, "I'm okay. I haven't done much fossil hunting though." Rose hesitated then spoke, "I saw the stallion you were talking about, but only for a second and then he disappeared. It was so strange."

Gus sat down on the rock next to Rose "What did you see?"

Rose hesitated again. "I only saw him for a few seconds before he knew I was there. Then he was gone. I went down to that small pool but I only saw a few hoof prints. I even tried to follow for a short distance." She pointed in the direction of the ghost horses she had just witnessed. "But, then this image appeared. It looked like a herd of horses, but no really, of course, it couldn't have been."

Gus responded. "Well, there could be a few more out here the government doesn't know about."

Rose interjected, "But these horses weren't alive! They looked like ghosts. It doesn't make sense!"

Gus, "Look, it's getting late. I don't like the looks of this sky. I should have warned you about how fast the weather can change out here. You can tell me more about what you saw when we get back to the diner." Immediately, Gus realized he had invited her to join him at his place. "If you want to, of course." Rose accepted, "I'd like that. I could use some reassurance I'm not seeing things!"

They both laughed as they got up and walked back to their trucks. They didn't see the helicopter off in the distance, but the stallion did. He was standing under an outcropping not far from where Gus and Rose had been. His eyes and ears were alerted to the sounds of the machine moving off into the waning light. He moved out from under the ledge and headed for the watering hole. He drank quickly and raised his head. This was his life now, staying ahead of his captors, but he would have help from now on.

Rose and Gus ran towards the diner as the storm hit. Bella was at the door barking at them to hurry up which caused them both to laugh. Gus took Rose's coat and headed back into the kitchen. Rose sat in one of the booths and watched the storm envelop the diner. Gus brought out two cups of hot coffee and sat opposite Rose. "I'll heat up something for us in a little bit."

Rose, "Thank you and thanks for alerting me to the storm. I was so caught up in what I had seen, I wasn't paying attention which isn't like me." "What do you think? Did I imagine what I saw?"

Gus, "I can't believe how lucky you were to see that old mustang the first time you go out there. As far as that other thing you saw, well, I don't have any answers. At least not right now."

Gus continued, "Maybe you should consider yourself fortunate to have seen what you did. I sure as hell would."

Smiling, Rose said, "Thanks for listening. I'm going to do a little research. After all, I'm a former professor. That's what we do."

Gus and Rose continued to talk. Rose told him about her previous life as a professor at a college in Arizona. She never had a family but was devoted to her students and spent a month every year working on archaeological digs. Gus compared her adventurous life to his in the high desert. Quiet but happy with many long time friends, something they both appreciated even if they didn't have families of their own. The skies had cleared as darkness descended on the diner. Gus spoke, "Had no idea it was getting so late."

Rose got up, "I should be getting back. Thank you again, it's been an eventful day."

"I appreciate your sharing what happened to you out there. Hope to have some answers for you real soon."

"You do believe I saw something."

"You bet I do." Gus walked her to her truck. He walked back to the diner with that same unsettled feeling. They had no idea how the events of the day would change their lives.

5

The following morning, Gus's friends came into the diner at their usual time for coffee and breakfast. They all gave Gus a nod and made themselves comfortable in their same booth. He pulled up a chair to join his friends. "How you fellas doin this morning?"

Daniel responded, "Okay, a little stiff from the cold." After a minute he asked, "Did that Rose woman have any luck out there yesterday?"

Gus replied, "Not much. She got a little spooked. A strange dust formation appeared for a few seconds. You know how you think you see things out there sometimes. But, she did see that old stallion that got away the other day. I sure hope that old boy makes it. Gus got up to get more coffee for his friends and make their usual potatoes and eggs. While he was behind the counter he picked up the snow globe. Suddenly, the image of the horse he saw in the trailer appeared. He was deep in thought when he heard Daniel.

"The helicopter was back yesterday. No luck though. I'll bet they're hoping he does the job for them by grabbing up the last of the horses that might be out there."

They all mumbled in agreement while shaking their heads.

Daniel asked, "Gus, what kind of things did she see?"

Gus replied, "Not sure, but I need to go see someone who might have some answers. Can you watch the place awhile? I shouldn't be too long.'

Daniel, laughing, "Sure, guess I can make some breakfast for these guys."

Gus laughed and headed for the door. He got into the truck after he let Bella jump in and the two started down the highway. Not far away the mustang moved through the low brush headed for the nearby trees. Gus pulled in front of an old adobe located on a nearby reservation. He and Bella got out of the truck and walked up to the front door. Samuel opened the door before Gus had a chance to knock. He greeted Gus and Bella warmly, "Come in my friend. I was just thinking about you. Missing that delicious pie of yours."

Gus laughing, "Anytime." He hesitated. "I was hoping you might have some time for me today. This can't wait until your next visit to the diner." Samuel showed Gus into his small living area. He gestured to a chair. Gus lowered himself into one of the two chairs in front of the fireplace. Samuel sat down opposite him. He allowed Gus to begin the conversation. "Samuel, you've been around here a long time and seen a lot of things. I thought you would be the right person to talk to." Samuel began to listen intently. "I met someone yesterday at my place, a woman, a geologist, who came out this way to look for fossils. I told her if she was lucky she might see our old mustang out there. Well, she did, but just for a second, then he was gone. Or at least she thought he was." Gus stopped. "Sorry I'm runnin on like this. Look, she said she saw something strange out there. She took her eyes off where she saw the horse and that's when she saw a small herd of horses, only they looked like ghosts not real horses. And I remember you telling me something similar to this a long time ago."

Samuel was quiet before he spoke, "Yes, I have seen them. I hope she wasn't frightened. It is an honor."

Gus, intrigued, "Refresh my memory. Does it have something to do with the mustang that's out there? Why would she see him and then witness such an event?" Gus then told Sam about his momentary encounter with the horse in the trailer. "I've never experienced anything like that. It was as if it was just me and that horse." Now, this woman Rose had this experience today. Is there a connection and does it involve this old mustang?"

While the two of them continued to discuss the experience in the desert, Rose had been busy doing research on the internet. She wanted to learn more about the area and the horses. She pulled up old newspaper clippings with the following headlines: LAST WILD HORSES TO BE ROUNDED UP; POTENTIAL DEVELOPERS HAVE EYE ON TWIN PEAKS; CATTLE RANCHERS WANT HORSES REMOVED; AND ANCIENT RELICS LOOTED IN CAVES. The last one caught her eye. She wondered what that had do to with the horses. It seems that some of them were of prehistoric horses. Rose sat for a long time staring at the headlines. Rose muttered, "So much for retirement." She had spent her adult life teaching at a university.

Having a family was always put off for the future, but that future caught up with her. Now she was retired. Her decision to venture to this part of the country had been spontaneous. Not a quality she had exhibited in the past. She was determined to find some answers.

Back at Samuel's house, he continued to tell Gus the history of the wild horses that lived in the area. "The wild ones that once lived in these mountains have all but disappeared. I saw those ghost horses once when I was a young boy. It was a time of great suffering for the horses. No laws to protect them. Now, even with the laws they are being driven off the land. Once they are gone this time will be over. Perhaps the spirit horses are looking out for him."

Gus responded immediately, "Well, I don't want to see that happen. You know, I can't seem to get these horses out of my head. I think I'm supposed to help some way. Samuel, there are a lot of folks interested in land around here, and these horses are in the way. This won't be easy." Gus and Sam sat quietly for a moment deep in thought. Bella could be heard barking outside. Gus continued, "I sometimes feel like I'm not finished living yet, just like these horses."

Samuel was deep in thought, but he responded, "Why don't you and that professor meet me in the next couple of days. I want to show you something."

Gus, "What have you got in mind?"

Samuel, "It has to do with the horses. Let's leave it at that for now. Do you remember that cave I showed you many years ago? We'll meet there."

Gus, "Now I am curious. I'll talk to her and get back to you. Thanks, Samuel." They shook hands and Samuel walked Gus to the door. He stood in the doorway while Gus and Bella walked to the truck. Sam stood there and watched the two of them until they were out of sight. He took a small carving of a horse from his pocket.

He spoke softly, "The time has finally come."

At the same time, Gus had stopped his pickup on the side of the highway. He looked off toward the nearby mountains deep in thought. He placed his hand on Bella's head. Looking into her eyes, he said, "I think our lives are about to change old girl. What do you think?" Bella barked in response and placed her head in his lap. Not far away the mustang could be seen, ears pricked forward as if he heard Samuel's voice.

6

The following morning Gus was working in the diner with a new energy. He greeted his friends as they came in for their usual morning coffee. First to speak was Daniel, "Is that you whistling, Gus?"

Gus, laughing, "I believe it is. Help yourselves to coffee. I have to finish sweeping these old floors." His friends settled into their usual spot and watched Gus finish up his chores. All the while they smiled to themselves. A few minutes later Gus had a question for them. "You fellas want to help me look for that old mustang today?"

Daniel nodded to the truck that had just pulled up outside the diner, "We may not have to." A moment later a middle-aged man in a government shirt entered the diner. He greeted Gus and his friends. Gus went over and noticed the name on his shirt.

"What can I get for you, Jim?"

"Just a coffee and an egg salad sandwich to go, if that's possible?" He asked. "No problem." Gus responded while he poured him coffee. He nodded toward the truck parked outside. "Are you still out there looking for horses?"

The conversations taking place in the diner went quiet. Gus's friends all turned around and gave the gentleman a once over. The mistrust of government officials is a part of life in this high country desert community.

"I guess I am. Not sure where the last of them are hiding though." Jim responded and after a long pause asked, "You've been around here a long time, you have any ideas?"

Gus replied with a mischievous grin, "Can't say that I do. How about you fellas? Any of you boys seen any wild horses in the vicinity?"

Gus's friends all shook their heads no in unison.

Jim noted the smile on Gus's face, "Would you tell me if you did?"

Gus, "Can't say that I would."

Gus went into the kitchen to see about the man's sandwich. When he returned, the gentleman was waiting at the register. He was holding the snow globe in his hand.

"Part of the job I have a problem with sometimes." Jim said quietly.

"Maybe the old stallion will outsmart all of you." Gus interjected.

"Maybe. He has so far. Or maybe his luck has run out." Jim replied.

The gentleman paid for his food and headed for the door. He turned just before leaving.

"You know, I did hear there might be a few left on the other side of the valley."

"I'll let them know. Thanks again." Jim answered with a slight smile on his face.

Gus approached his friends, "What do you think? Will they follow my suggestion?"

Gus sat down and pulled out a piece of paper and pencil from his pocket and began to draw the area where he last saw the mustang.

Gus, "This is where Rose last saw

the old boy. Our problem is how do we keep an eye on him without drawing attention to what we're doin?"

Daniel, "Maybe we should keep an eye on them instead of him. Find ways to keep them occupied."

"Now I like how you're thinking. Boys, let's see what we can come up with" Gus said enthusiastically.

While the boys were planning their next move, Rose was out looking for fossils or so she had convinced herself. Around her neck were a pair of binoculars in case the horse showed up again. She had not been able to get him out of her mind. While she looked through them she spotted Gus and his friend Daniel. They were pointing in the direction of a mountain range in the distance. She looked in the same direction. A helicopter was visible in the distance. She didn't know at the time that Gus had pointed the government in the wrong direction. While Rose is watching the helicopter uneasily, Gus and Daniel are enjoying the sight of it searching in the wrong area.

Daniel, "It will give us some time to figure this out."

They continued to watch the helicopter circle a few more times unaware that Rose had been watching them. At the same time, the mustang had found himself a place to hide while he too watched the machine searching for him.

7

Rose approached the entrance to the diner. She could see Gus through the front window. A slight smile appeared on her face. She was looking forward to seeing him. Maybe he had some answers for her because she had lots of questions. She walked into the diner and saw that Gus was busy cleaning. He looked up and smiled.

"Did you find any fossils?"

"Yes, a few, but I also saw you and another man out there through my binoculars. Why were you pointing at the helicopter and why was it out there?" Rose asked with some concern.

Gus chuckled, "They were looking in the wrong place." He paused, "Would you be interested in meeting an old friend of mine. I told him about your experience the other day. He may have some answers."

Well, I would love to hear an explanation for what I saw if there is one. Can't get it out of my head. I think my looking for fossils today was just an excuse. I was really looking for answers". Rose replied.

Gus leaned on his broom. "All right then. I'll set up a time. Why don't you come by tomorrow, I should have something by early afternoon."

Rose picked up the snow globe. "I'll see you tomorrow."

She put down the snow globe and paused a moment before leaving. "You know, this place was on the list of places to see. Not at the top, maybe number five. I'm very glad I changed my mind. It's almost serendipitous if I believed in such a thing."

With a twinkle in his eye, Gus responded, "Perhaps by the time your visit is over you just might believe in such things. This place has a way of changing you."

"After what I've seen it already has Gus. See you tomorrow."

Rose exited the diner, but not before giving a final wave to Gus and patting Bella on the head. Gus spent a long moment watching Rose get into her truck and head down the highway. With a smile on his face he once again began to whistle as he went about his work.

Samuel also saw the helicopter off in the distance. He had been following the path the stallion had taken. He spoke softly, "You're a wise one. Keeping ahead of them, are you?" He stood quietly for a long time. He appreciated what this horse was up against. He knew the odds weren't good for him. He remained there until the afternoon light began to fade. There would be difficult days ahead and he must prepare himself if he and his friends were to succeed.

That evening in the diner Gus and Bella were having a late dinner. He gave her a warm smile, "You know old girl, I think I need to spruce this place up a bit if we're going to have company tomorrow. I might just ask Rose to stay for dinner. What do you think of that?" Bella gave a loud bark in agreement. At the same time that Gus is having dinner alone, the mustang can be heard moving in the dark. His loneliness echoed by the sound of his hooves. He moved alone through the brush and rocks until he found a safe place even if for a short time. Tomorrow he would continue to search for other wild ones who might still be out there.

8

The old stallion had moved from his secure place. He sniffed the morning air. He began to nicker gently and moved off into the new day. At the same time, Daniel drove down the road and came upon a government truck and decided to follow. After a short time, the truck turned into a canyon area. He pulled over and walked up to the top of the ridge. Down below he could see several men setting up a wild horse trap. Daniel murmured, "Well, I'll be damned. They aren't wasting any time." After taking a few pictures, he got back into his truck and drove slowly from the scene until he was back on the highway. He had a lot to tell Gus when he got back.

Rose parked her truck in front of the diner. She was eager to see Gus. She walked quickly and entered the diner. Gus gave her a warm smile. Before he had a chance to say hello she asked, "Are we ready to go? I'm looking forward to meeting your friend."

Gus, "Sure am. It's pretty quiet

around here. No reason why I can't close up for a while. My friends know where I keep the key." He paused, "I thought we might come back later and have some dinner. Would that work for you?"

Rose responded enthusiastically, "It most definitely would work for me and thank you."

Gus hung the closed sign on the door as they proceeded to his truck. Bella was already waiting. He opened the door and Bella hopped in and over the seat into the space behind Gus. Gus opened the door for Rose before she had a chance to do it herself. She smiled, "I think this is going to be a wonderful day." Once they were inside the truck and on their way, she asked, "Where are we meeting your friend?"

Gus proceeded to tell her about Samuel, "There's an old cave not far from here. For some reason, he wanted us to meet there. His full name is Samuel Running Deer. He's been living in this area for a long time. He knows the history of this place and he's seen a lot; some good some bad. When it comes to the wild horses mostly bad."

Rose, "This gets more interesting every minute. To think I came here to look for a bunch of old rocks." She looked over and gave Gus a big smile.

Sam was sitting in front of a campfire when they pulled up outside the cave entrance. He waved to Gus and Rose as they parked the truck. Bella began to bark excitedly. Sam stood up and gestured to Rose to sit down and offered her some tea.

Rose greeted him, "Thank you. It's good to meet you. I can't tell you how much I'm looking forward to this evening." She looked up at the sky, "It's going to be a beautiful night."

They spent the next few minutes drinking their tea and enjoying the deepening evening sky.

After a few minutes Gus spoke, "The conditions are good for a lunar rainbow. What do you think?"

"That would be a good sign." Samuel paused, "Let me show you something inside the cave, Rose."

They proceeded into the cave with Sam holding a lantern. It cast long shadows across the walls of the cave. The ancient horse drawings jumped out from the shadows. Rose walked up to the drawings and examined them closely. While she traced the lines with her fingertips, she saw the image of the mustang. She suddenly drew her hand back. "I just saw an image of the mustang. It was so clear as if he was here."

Sam spoke quietly, "He is here, along with all the others. The horses have been here for a very long time. My people have a story on how the horse came to be with our ancestors. Because you have now seen the ghost horses, I think you will receive it with an open heart."

They moved outside to sit around the fire. Samuel took his place and began the creation story. In preparation he took a small figurine of a horse from his pocket and held it in his hand. A slow murmur came from deep within him. The air began to change and the lantern seemed to glow brighter. The small horse in his hand came alive. Gus and Rose looked on in amazement. Unknowing to Rose, Gus had reached for her hand. Suddenly, the wind picked up outside the cave entrance. Sam could be heard chanting the names given to the horses over time. They remained riveted to the scene before them. The night sky was filled with shooting stars. When the story was finished, the horse was still, just a small figurine in his hand. Their attention was drawn to the fire as an image of the ghost horses could be seen. Rose let go of Gus's hand to gesture towards the image.

"It's them! That is what I saw the other day. Can you see it, Gus?"

"I sure can." Gus said quietly.

As quickly as the image appeared, it was gone. Everyone remained quiet. Only the sound of the fire and various night sounds could be heard.

"How is what I just saw possible?" Rose questioned excitedly.

Gus flashed back to his earlier contact with the mustang in the trailer. "Something very important is happening and it involves this old stallion, but I don't know what we can do."

Samuel addressed Rose, "You're a witness to something powerful. You must remember this and tell his story."

Rose stared at the fire for a short while before she spoke, "My life up till now has been about the study of rocks. Samuel, you breathed life into them." Rose looked at Gus and squeezed his hand.

Gus continued to hold her hand while he spoke, "Let's go. Samuel, please stay close by. Don't know what the next few days will bring." They got up from the fire and started to leave. They turned around and reached for Samuel to thank him without words.

As the couple drove down the high desert road, they witnessed something extraordinary happening in the night sky. Gus pulled over and both of them got out of the truck.

Rose pointed upward, "What is that?"

A rainbow had appeared. A sweep of stardust appeared within pastel bands of light; pink, lavender, yellow and blue. It was an amazing sight.

"Haven't seen a lunar rainbow before?" He asked Rose.

She exclaimed, "I've heard of them but never saw one until now! What a night! What's next?"

Gus responded, "I think we're about to find out real soon."

At the same time Gus and Rose witnessed the lunar rainbow, another magical moment took place in a nearby meadow. The mustang was visible in the light of the moon. He moved slowly across the meadow, but then his pace began to quicken. Suddenly, a mare and her foal appeared at the far end of the meadow. A gentle nickering could be heard.   Eventually, the foal trotted up to the stallion and, he in turn, slowly lowered his head. The mare approached and they touched each other's necks. The foal looked up, and excitedly began to run circles around them. The loneliness that had followed the old mustang had been replaced with the joy of a family, even if it was just this one night.

Gus and Rose returned to his truck and continued down the road towards the diner. Both were quiet, having spent the evening witnessing events that would change their lives forever. They entered the diner and Gus gestured for her to have a seat while he went into the kitchen to prepare dinner. Before Rose sat down, she picked up the snow globe from the counter. Rose looked at the globe intently. She reached down to pat Bella's head, "This has been an unforgettable night. I came looking for fossils and found so much more."

Gus entered from the back carrying two plates of food, with a treat for Bella tucked under his arm. He set the plates down and emptied the treat into Bella's bowl.

Rose was pleasantly surprised. "It looks wonderful. How did you do that so quickly?"

Gus smiled shyly, "I have a confession. I had hoped you might join me for dinner. Hope that wasn't being too presumptuous of me."

Rose returned the smile, "Not at all. It's lovely, Gus."

Just as Gus was about to sit down, the phone rang. A look of concern crossed his face as he listened intently to the caller. He put down the phone and once again sat down for dinner.

"Is there anything wrong, Gus?"

"That was Daniel. He saw a horse trap being set up not too far from here. Looks like they haven't given up on the old boy."

Rose protested, "How do we stop it? After all we've seen tonight, I can't believe he could be captured."

Gus, "I think we should pay these folks a visit."

Rose nodded her head in agreement. She knew they didn't have much time if they were to save this last wild horse. After tonight, he would occupy her every waking moment. She kept thinking about what Samuel had said to her. She was to remember and tell his story. Rose wasn't sure how she was supposed to accomplish such a request, but after seeing the ghost horses nothing seemed impossible.

    While Gus and Rose enjoyed their late night dinner together, Samuel continued his vigil around the campfire. The howling of coyotes could be heard in the distance. There was much to do and little time left. Not far from the cave, the stallion, mare and foal could be seen galloping over the meadow underneath the still bright moon. Once again, he had a family.

9

The next morning Gus and Daniel's dogs could be seen sitting outside the diner staring into the window. A serious conversation was going on between Gus, Rose and Daniel.

Gus, "There's no way we can stop these guys once they figure out his location. Our only chance is to keep them away from the old boy."

Rose, "What do you suggest? You and Daniel know this area so I'll go along with any ideas you have."

Just as they were talking, the government man Gus spoke to on a previous occasion came in. He acknowledged them and sat down in one of the booths. The group immediately stopped talking. Gus got up and walked over to him. Gus decided to have a polite conversation with the man and perhaps get some information at the same time.

"What can I get you this fine day?"

"If I could have a turkey sandwich and a cup to coffee to go that would be great."

"Sure thing. I guess you guys are still looking for more horses. I thought you would have them all by now."

"Couple left. Not supposed to leave until it's done. Don't suppose you've seen them lately."

"What harm can a couple of horses do? Plenty of space out there."

"Like I said before, just doing my job. Don't always like it."

"And like I said before, we haven't seen any. I'll be getting that order for you."

Gus went back to the kitchen while Rose and friends talked quietly. The government man pretended to be checking his phone for messages, but was actually taking photos of the group and sent them back to the office. Gus came out of the kitchen with the man's order and noticed the man had taken pictures. He pretended not to notice and began whistling.

"Thanks," while he quickly put away his phone. "Well, I'd better be going." He handed Gus the money and refused the change.

"Well alright and thanks. Appreciate the business."

Gus watched as the man got into his truck. He proceeded over to his friends after the man had pulled out of the parking lot. "We have to be careful. That gentleman took pictures of you just now. They must think we know something about the old mustang."

Everyone watched the truck pull out onto the highway. They continued to watch until it was no longer visible.

Gus interrupted the silence, "I don't know about you folks, but I can feel what that old stallion is going through. He just wants to be left alone and live in peace for his last years." Gus paused and then continued, "We'll all go down fighting. Are we agreed? Samuel wants to help too."

They all looked at one another and nodded in agreement. From outside the diner Bella barked her approval.

The mustang moved cautiously through a grove of trees. He pricked his ears forward listening intently. Not far away, a pickup could be seen with the same government official who had been at the diner. He had a pair of binoculars. He continued to scan the countryside hoping to catch a glimpse of the elusive horse. He was unaware the stallion was nearby. He put the binoculars away, mumbled to himself and returned to the truck. It wasn't going to be easy but he had a job to do. The stallion remained motionless until the danger had moved away. He kept to the trees until he knew it was safe.

On the following day, Gus, Samuel and Rose are together at Samuel's home seated in front of the fireplace. They haven't seen him since that extraordinary evening a few days ago.

Rose, "Good to see you again. Still thinking about the other night."

Sam nodded his head and handed her the figurine he had held in his hand while in the cave, Rose grasped it tightly in her hands.

"No other gift could mean as much as this. Thank you."

Gus had been quiet up till then, "Samuel, it looks like they're setting a trap for him. We're going to try and delay them."

"It may not be possible to stop what is meant to be." he responded.

"We have to try. He deserves

more than what they'll do to him. He belongs in the wild for as long as he got. At least we can disrupt them for a while. Maybe they'll get tired and move on."

Rose asked, "What have you got in mind?"

I don't want to bring the government down on you, so the less you know the better. But, I might need you for something else."

"Anything. I've fallen for that guy."

Gus smiled, "Just suppose you were to find some real interesting old artifacts out there. This round up might be causing some undue harm to these objects. If you get my intentions here. Maybe Samuel here can come up with something real old and valuable to his people."

Samuel smiling, "I think I can help with that."

Sam pulled out a map from the bookcase and spread it out on the table. The three began pointing out possible locations where one might find such an artifact. Gus pointed out an area while Rose and Sam looked at each and nodded in agreement. Rose had thirty years of experience so she could make the whole thing look real and Sam had the artifact.

Rose, "Let's do it."

10

The next evening Gus and Bella could be seen moving around the horse trap which had been set up to capture the mustang. Gus carefully loosened several of the posts. He whispered to Bella, "These won't hold you. What do you think old girl?" Bella seemed to know that she couldn't bark so she wagged her tail and jumped up on Gus and licked his face.

"I guess you approve." Gus moved quickly into the trees with Bella right behind him. He was unaware that up on the hill overlooking the site below, but well within the trees, the old stallion watched. He nickered softly.

While Gus worked on the trap, Rose was at Samuel's house looking over some very ancient Indian artifacts. She smiled and looked at him while she held two of the pieces.

"I think these will work just fine. I'll file the paperwork tomorrow. Should hold them off for a while, at least for a few days, at least."

Samuel nodded in agreement. Rose

packed up the artifacts handling them very carefully. She knew how valuable they were. They shook hands and Rose went out into the desert night. There was much to do and she had little time.

The next day Rose met Gus and Daniel at the diner. When she approached the booth, she overheard Daniel, "I like the sound of this. About time we did something."

Gus smiled at Rose and made room for her to join them.

"I've been telling Daniel that we need to have those government men think we're carrying on the way we always have around here. I've been doing some fixing up to this place.

How about a little get together?"

Daniel enthusiastically, "Let me know when and I'll get the word out. Need me to bring anything?"

Gus "I'll get back to you. Who knows, maybe a couple of those government men will stop by. Real casual way to get information."

Daniel, "Perhaps I should stop by those traps and put out an invitation. Give me a chance to snoop around a little bit."

Rose smiling, "Well, I've got to get an early start if I'm going to find some old fossils. See you tomorrow."

Gus, "We'll be right here. Let us know how it goes and be careful out there. They're watching us. That much we do know."

Gus watched as Rose waved goodbye from her truck. He continued to watch through the window of the diner until her truck disappeared down the highway.

Daniel, "She's a real interesting woman. Would she be one of the reasons you're fixing this place up?"

Gus looked directly at Daniel. A slight smile crossed his face. "She sure is. Didn't think I'd ever agree to a statement like that." He paused, "Okay, I've got a party to plan."

He and Daniel got up and gave each other a nod. There was much to do if their plan was going to work. There was a lightness to their step as they proceeded to the next phase of their journey to save this special horse. Gus watched as Daniel drove away from the diner. He wondered what the mustang was doing right now.

While Rose pursued her mission of planting an artifact, the mustang was galloping across the desert. He came to a grove of junipers where the mare and her foal had hidden themselves. They greeted each other with soft nickers and gentle bites. The foal stood nearby, but soon began running around the couple, kicking up its back legs. The three have survived another day. Meanwhile, Rose stood outside her truck holding a small canvas bag. She checked through her binoculars.

Rose, speaking to herself, "This looks like a good spot for my discovery."

She moved the dirt and rocks around with her small shovel. She reached into her bag to remove the samples she received from Sam and placed one of them into the ground. Rose decided to keep the other ones to show to the authorities. She marked the spot with a small post. A small smile appeared on her face as she looked out onto the surrounding landscape. She headed back to her truck and called Gus before leaving to present her findings to the proper agency.

In the meantime, Daniel visited the

still empty trap. A man in uniform was standing by one of the corrals. He approached him with a friendly wave.

"Hey, how you doing?" I see you still haven't found that horse yet."

Daniel moved around the trap while he spoke to the now suspicious guard. He gently tested the posts to see if they were still loose. He did so while he distracted the government man with conversation.

"Look, Gus has been fixing up his place and wanted to celebrate with a little party. You guys are more than welcome."

Daniel and the government man shook hands and parted company. After Daniel left, the employee continued to watch Daniel's truck with his arms crossed over his chest.

Speaking to himself, "We just might take you up on that invitation."

While Daniel is out issuing invitations, Gus is busy with a paintbrush. A new coat of paint had been sorely needed. Bella watched from her bed in the corner.

"Well, girl, what do you think? Amazing what a fresh coat of paint can do. Next, I've got to scrub this floor and the booths. Need to hang some lights. Too damn dark in here."

Gus surveyed his establishment with his hands on his hips. Bella joined him. He reached down to pat her head and she barked her approval.

11

Strings of new lights invited those parked in front of the diner. All pointed in amazement before entering. Inside was a warm and inviting scene. Rose arrived next. She was dressed in a floral skirt with a jacket and low heels. Samuel had also just arrived and waved to her in greeting. "It's good to see some life in this place."

Rose, smiling, "It was a good day. I believe you could say mission accomplished. I have to say there have been lots of good days since I drove up to this place."

Samuel, "The time was right for you to be here."

"I didn't realize I had become so comfortable in my old life. I like this new me."

Samuel held the door for her. Greetings could be heard from inside. Outside a few tumbleweeds rolled down the highway. Bella and friends chased them barking furiously. The evening sky seemed to go on forever in this high desert community. The only lights other than the stars were the warm lights coming from the diner. The party was the first in many years, but it would also be an opportunity to finalize their plan to help save the horse who had become so special to them.

The party is well under way when a government man entered the diner. A friendly greeting met him, but he was interested in talking to only one person that night. He made his way over to Rose. He was unaware that Gus kept a watchful eye.

"May I call you Rose? I just received a call earlier this evening regarding some artifacts you found not too far from here. I realize we have to follow certain protocols when a discovery like that is made."

"Yes, you may call me Rose and I'll be filing the necessary paperwork tomorrow."

"Quite a coincidence, don't you think? Close to our capture site. This may slow things up a bit."

At this point, Gus came over having heard parts of the conversation.

"Not giving up, huh? Why bother with just one or two horses? What harm can they do?"

"Those are the orders." While he spoke those words, he picked up the snow globe. "It looks like their time is up in these parts." He turned to Rose, "I hope to hear from you real soon."

He placed the snow globe on the counter and moved toward the door.

As the door closed behind him, Gus took Rose to one of the empty tables.

"Care to share what you two were talking about?"

"He knew about my discovery. He's suspicious, but I think I can string them along for a bit."

"That's what we need just a little more time. Don't know how this is going to play out, but sure do appreciate your help."

"Gus, I never realized my life had become so predictable until I came upon this place. I guess I have you and that horse to thank."

"You know, I feel the same. This whole thing has given me a reason to get up in the morning. Now, how about having some of my homemade chili? I got pie, too!"

　　　Gus gently put his hand on Rose's arm and gestured gallantly for her to sit down. Rose took her seat while she looked up at him. They both smiled at one another. Their attention to one another wasn't lost on his friends who looked on with a gentle knowing. Their friend had been alone a long time. It was nice to see him smile. In fact, he had been smiling a lot these days. They all continued into the evening enjoying themselves. Before the evening was over, they all raised their glasses to toast a new day for the diner and to Gus. Even the dogs who had been barking and playing in the lot outside seemed to know that something had changed. Not far from the diner, the stallion and mare could be seen nuzzling each other. It had been a good night.

12

A few days later, the government man looked through his binoculars while he stood outside his truck. He had just about given up looking for that lone stallion when he spotted movement in a group of trees. "Well, what do you know. So, you found some company."

His eyes remained focused on the stallion, mare and foal. He immediately got on his cell phone and climbed back into his truck. What he didn't realize that someone was watching him. Rose kept her binoculars focused on the scene before her. After the man drove off, she too jumped into her truck and drove off.

The government man drove up to the horse trap. He approached the men who had been making the final preparations.

"Looks like the old man has a mare and foal with him. Have a bit more work ahead than we expected."

Their attention is diverted to the pickup which had pulled up to the trap. Rose got out and waved a large manila envelope.

"Hello gentlemen. I have a letter addressing the issue of the artifacts I found. By now you probably have your own copy."

"We have already filed an appeal. Should only be a couple of days before we finish up here." He paused before he addressed her again. "Ma'am you're on the wrong side of this. We have a job to do and we're going to do it. You might want to tell that to your friends."

Rose responded, "We'll see about that. Good talking with you."

They watched her drive away, "C'mon boys we've got work to do."

Rose decided to go out and look for the horse. She parked the truck and brought her binoculars to look toward the now familiar watering hole. She sat down on a nearby rock and looked pensively into the distance. Just as she was about to give up she saw a dust cloud in the distance. An image materialized, but only for a moment. Just then the mustang appeared in the same area.

Rose voiced her concern, "Why are you with those horses, old man? Is it your time like Samuel suggested?"

Rose remained silent until the horse disappeared into the waning light. She got up, dusted her clothes off and put the binoculars away. After getting into the truck, she drove quickly down the highway. She was anxious to see

Gus.

Rose pulled up outside Samuel's house. She got out and waved to Gus and Sam who had been talking as she approached.

She nodded to Gus, "Hi, I didn't know you'd be here. I was near the watering hole where I saw those ghost horses. I saw them again, but this time I had a bad feeling."

Samuel spoke quietly, "The old stallion is prepared to see this through. We will stay close. I don't think it will be much longer."

He addressed them both, "You have done what you could."

Rose, "Did the two of you know that he has a mare and foal with him now? Doesn't this complicate things?"

Gus responded excitedly, "It sure does. Now it's even more important that we try to protect him. He's got a family. We have to keep a close eye on these guys until we know when Rose's injunction is lifted. Samuel, meet Rose and I at the diner tomorrow morning."

He watched the two of them drive away. Events were taking shape that none of them could prevent, but he didn't want to disappoint them. Sometime later that evening, Samuel came upon the horses. He began to utter a prayer. They pointed their ears in his direction but didn't move.

In the night sky a meteor was visible. Both human and horses watched its trail across the night sky.

13

The following morning everyone involved in this mission to save the horses had gathered at the diner. Doughnuts and coffee were served. There was much discussion while they observed various maps strewn about on the tables. Rose took a phone call. A look of concern crossed her face as she put the phone back in her bag.

Gus observed her expression,

"That wasn't the news we were hoping for was it?"

Rose, "They got the injunction overturned. Sure didn't waste any time. I should have tried harder."

Gus, "It was a long shot. We have to move on to Plan B."

Everyone looked at Gus.

Daniel inquired, "I don't recall a Plan B, Gus. What might that be?"

Gus, "That's what is great about a Plan B. It can be anything. Now let's figure this out."

While a new plan was being drawn up, a helicopter had taken off from the horse trap. The three government men had moved the horse trailer into place. The final preparations have been made for their capture. In another direction, the mustang can be seen moving behind the mare and foal. They are headed in the direction of Samuel's place. At the same time, Sam had his eyes focused on the nearby hills. He saw the horses were headed towards him.

Samuel, "Well, I'll be. You are showing us the way." He raised his hand, "This we can do for you."

Once the mustang left his family, he began galloping towards the nearby hills. Samuel watched him move quickly away towards an uncertain future.

Meanwhile, Rose and Gus are at the diner. Gus on the phone, "Okay, Sam we'll wait for you." He hung up the phone and turned to Rose.

Rose, "What's going on?"

Gus, "Samuel is on his way over. Has something for us."

Daniel walked into the diner. He approached the two of them with a very concerned look on his face. "Gus, this doesn't look good."

Daniel sat down opposite them, "I was watching the corrals. Lots of activity. Helicopter in the air. I think this is it."

The group sat together and waited for Sam to show up. Gus got up and got coffee for the three of them. Moments later, Samuel pulled up to the diner. He acknowledged them before he sat down. Gus didn't waste any time as everyone was anxious to hear what he had to say.

Gus, "What have you got for us?"

Samuel, "It's happening soon. The stallion is going to have it his way."

Gus, "So you're saying there is nothing left for us to do."

"We are part of this, but it must unfold according to the old ones."

Rose interjected, "I'm feeling helpless, but I will do my part. I've already started writing his story. Don't have an ending yet."

Daniel asked, "Do you know where he is, Samuel?"

"He's headed towards Twin Peaks. That is where we must go too."

An hour later, the helicopter was flying over the area leading towards Twin Peaks. It was flying low and circled a specific area. Below, the old stallion was galloping across the high desert floor. The helicopter was following very close. His breathing was labored, but he continued to run, but he did not turn in the direction the pilots wanted him to go.

Pilot, "Can't you get him to turn in the other direction? If he keeps this up he'll break down out here. That will bring us nothing but trouble."

The co-pilot was looking through his binoculars. "I don't see any sign of the other two, do you?" Those folks up on the ridge are watching this whole thing. It's going to hit the fan."

He had run into a ravine, but managed to go up the side and onto the open desert floor. He was now limping badly.

An emotional Gus, "Did you see that? Damn, he's hurt bad. He never gave up Rose, he never gave up."

As Gus spoke, the helicopter turned back the way they came.

Rose, "Look at that, they're leaving him out here like that."

Gus, "They'll be sending people out to check on him and cover their backsides at the same time. Probably put him down. But, we're here and we saw it all."

Rose asked, "Is there anything we can do for him?"

Samuel, "Nothing, it's done. We must witness the end of his story."

The legendary stallion continued to limp towards an approaching cloud of dust. Within the image were the shapes of horses enveloped in light.

Rose, "Do you see that? Oh God, I think I know what's going to happen."

The mustang moved into the light He was now one with the ghost horses. The ghost herd moved away and disappeared into the desert taking the mustang with them. A quiet descended over the area. The group who witnessed the extraordinary event remained silent. It was as if time had stopped.

Samuel spoke quietly, "It is finished."

A low sound can be heard from him. Gus and Rose continued to stare towards the horizon. He reached out to her as she grabbed his hand.

Samuel was the first to speak, "We must go. I have something to show you."

Rose responded tearfully, "I don't know if I can move. We won't forget this. We can't forget this."

"You have much to do Rose. Now you can tell his story."

The group moved away from the scene below. As they approached the truck, Rose turned around. "They'll be here soon looking for him and his family."

Samuel, "They will never find

them. Come we must go."

As the group got into Gus's truck, Rose looked back and saw an iridescent light still visible in the distance.

On a bluff overlooking Samuel's place, Rose, Gus and Daniel could be seen looking into a small valley.

Daniel, "Thanks for inviting me. Still can't grasp what you told me about the old stallion. But, it sure makes a great story."

Rose, "That's what I'm hoping for." She paused, "Look at that. Looks like we've got a different ending."

In the valley below, the mare and foal could be seen grazing peacefully.

14

ONE YEAR LATER

Daniel entered the diner and nodded to Gus and Rose who had just emerged from the kitchen. Daniel gave her a smile. Visible on the shelf next to the register are several copies of the book, Legend, the Story of An American Mustang. Alongside them are several snow globes just like the original one Gus has had for years.

Daniel spoke to Rose, "Have I told you lately how nice it is to see you here on a regular basis?"

Rose laughing, "Just a dozen times."

"Have you made it legal yet?"

Gus wandered over to join the conversation.

"As a matter of fact, we did. Stood on the cliff overlooking the watering hole. Rose, myself and the Good Lord."

Daniel gave them both big hugs, "Doesn't get any more legal than that."

Samuel entered with his daughter and granddaughter. They are greeted with a warm welcome.

Gus, "Good to see you again. Rose and I just made some delicious apple pie. (He winked at Rose) We're celebrating Rose's new book."

Rose laughing, "I was never much of a cook until I met Gus. Hope it's good."

She noticed Dove, Sam's granddaughter, looking at the books, "How about an autographed copy?"

Dove smiled shyly, "Yes, very much."

Rose signed one of the books and handed it to Dove, who clutched it to her chest.

"Thank you. Grandfather takes us out to see his family once in a while. We don't get close. Don't want them to leave the valley. Rose gave her a hug, "They're safe and that's all that matters. Now, let's all have that pie."

Everyone agreed. It is evident by the joy on their faces that there is much to celebrate.

Gus, "Does everyone have a glass of something? How about a toast to one amazing horse. May he live forever in our hearts and in this land."

Outside the diner, Dove sat on the porch with the book in her lap and Bella by her feet. She turned the last page and read it aloud, "The young horse is seen standing on an outcropping gazing at the distant mountains." She closed the book and held it close to her.

In a valley not far away, the young horse picked her head up and looked towards the mountains and whinnied softly .

Epilogue

Where once vast herds of mustangs ran free, there is now silence. A symbol of freedom, they are now powerless in their plight. The land the wild horses called home is disappearing, and although protected by law, their numbers continue to diminish. Soon the thunder of their hooves will be no more than mere whispers upon the wind.

LEGEND
The Story of an American Mustang

Deborah Ellsworth

Deborah Ellsworth

ISBN-10: 1986738175
ISBN-13: 978-1986738170

Made in the USA
Las Vegas, NV
10 February 2022

43468442R00075